Ladybird books are widely available, but in case of
difficulty may be ordered by post or telephone from:

Ladybird Books – Cash Sales Department
Littlegate Road Paignton Devon TQ3 3BE
Telephone 01803 554761

A catalogue record for this book is available
from the British Library

Published by Ladybird Books Ltd Loughborough Leicestershire UK
LADYBIRD and the device of a Ladybird are trademarks of Ladybird Books Ltd

DISNEP

THE ARISTOCATS

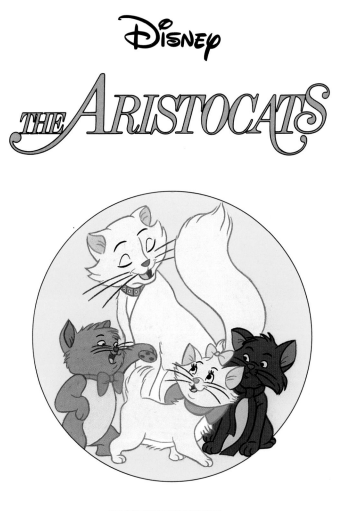

Madame Adelaide was a kind, gracious and very wealthy old lady who lived in Paris at the turn of the century.

She shared her beautiful home with her cat, Duchess, and Duchess's kittens, Toulouse, Berlioz and Marie.

These were not ordinary cats. They were clever, artistic *Aristocats*. Toulouse was a talented painter, Berlioz played the piano and Marie planned to be a great opera singer.

One day Madame asked her lawyer to visit. "It's time to make my will," she told him. "I wish to leave everything to my beloved cats. For as long as they live, they will be cared for by Edgar, my faithful butler. When the cats are gone, my fortune will go to him."

Downstairs in the kitchen, Edgar was listening to every word. He was furious that he would have to wait for the cats to die before he got any money.

He decided to get rid of the cats as soon as he could. That evening he put some sleeping pills in their milk.

"Here you are," said Edgar, setting down the bowls. "My speciality – crème de la crème à la Edgar!"

The cats and their friend, Roquefort the mouse, lapped up every drop. The cats just managed to stagger to their basket before they fell into a deep sleep.

That night, when Madame was in bed, Edgar sneaked the cats' basket out to his motorbike. He planned to take Duchess and the kittens to the countryside and drown them!

Near a farm, just outside Paris, two dogs leapt out at the motorbike, giving Edgar a terrible fright.

As he swerved and went rolling down an embankment, the cats' basket tumbled out of the sidecar. Edgar left it where it was. All he wanted to do was to get home safely before the dogs attacked him!

Next morning the cats crawled out of their basket.

"Where are we, Mama?" asked Marie.

"And how did we get here?" asked Berlioz, looking round in confusion.

"I don't know, darlings," said Duchess, "but don't be frightened. Everything is going to be all right!"

As Duchess wondered what to do, an alley cat strolled by. He was singing, "I'm Abraham Delacey… Giuseppe Casey… Thomas O'Malley the Alley Cat!" He gave a friendly smile when he saw Duchess and the kittens, and they smiled back at him.

When they told O'Malley they were lost, he immediately offered to help them get back to Paris.

Duchess and the kittens followed their new
friend along a railway line. The kittens
raced ahead across a bridge. Suddenly
they heard a train whistle.

"Careful, children!" Duchess warned. But
it was too late. The *whoosh* of the train
knocked Marie off the bridge and into the
river far below.

Without a moment's hesitation, O'Malley dived in and rescued the terrified kitten.

All that day and into the night the little band of cats trudged on. By the time they reached Paris, they were exhausted.

It was still a long way to Madame's house, so O'Malley invited Duchess and the kittens to spend the night at his home.

But when they got there, they found that O'Malley already had visitors – a group of alley cats, led by his friend, Scat Cat, were playing jazz music. The whole building seemed to be swinging to the beat!

The kittens forgot their tiredness and joined in the fun. Berlioz helped play the piano, Toulouse kept time to the music, and Marie sang at the top of her voice.

Even Duchess couldn't resist joining in too. She and O'Malley danced happily until midnight.

Later, when the jazz band had left and the kittens were asleep, O'Malley and Duchess sat together in the moonlight.

"I wish you didn't have to go," O'Malley said to Duchess. "And the kittens – they need a sort of… well… a father, don't they?"

Duchess wished she could stay too. But she had to think of Madame.

"I'm sorry," she told O'Malley sadly. "We must go home tomorrow."

Next morning O'Malley escorted Duchess
and the kittens home. As the kittens
miaowed at the door, Duchess and
O'Malley said goodbye.

"I'll never forget
you, Thomas
O'Malley,"
said Duchess,
fondly.

Edgar was in the kitchen, celebrating his victory with a bottle of champagne, when he heard the kittens.

"It can't be them!" he exclaimed. "It isn't fair!" He ran upstairs to stop them before Madame realised they were back.

As the cats came through the door, a sack came down over their heads. Edgar took the sack out to the barn and put it in a trunk that was being sent to Timbuktu.

Roquefort the mouse, who had come out to welcome the cats, saw everything. He dashed outside and caught up with O'Malley.

"Duchess and the kittens in trouble?" said O'Malley. "I'm on my way! But I'll need help. Get Scat Cat and the alley cats." And he told Roquefort how to find them.

Roquefort was scared of meeting these strange cats all by himself – but he would do anything to rescue his friends. He scurried off as quickly as he could.

At first the alley cats teased Roquefort and threatened to eat him, but at the mention of O'Malley's name they all agreed to help.

"Follow me!" cried Roquefort, as he led Scat Cat and the alley cats to Madame's house.

By the time Roquefort returned, Edgar
had trapped O'Malley in the barn with
a pitchfork. The alley cats stormed
in, hissing, biting and scratching.

While the cats dealt with Edgar, Roquefort
managed to undo the padlock on the
trunk. As soon as O'Malley had helped
Duchess and the kittens to get out, the
alley cats shoved Edgar inside.

In a few minutes the delivery van arrived
for the trunk, and Edgar was on his way
to Timbuktu!

Madame Adelaide was thrilled to have Duchess and the kittens back. She was also delighted to meet O'Malley. "He's so handsome," she said.

Madame decided to keep O'Malley in the family and set up a home for all the alley cats of Paris. From then on, all cats would be treated as special, wonderful *Aristocats*!